MW01603053

NONE THE RISER

RAISED AND GLAZED COZY MYSTERIES,
BOOK 20

EMMA AINSLEY

SUMMER PRESCOTT BOOKS PUBLISHING

CHAPTER ONE

"I've never understood the point of standing in the middle of a stream, throwing a string at the fish over and over, hoping one of them is dumb enough to open their mouths and bite down," Orson Hawley muttered.

"What on earth are you going on about?" Maggie Sharpe asked her oldest employee. She stood in front of the store room and tossed her soiled apron into the hamper just inside the door.

"Have you been out there?" Orson asked her. He pointed toward the swinging door that separated the kitchen and dining area of Dogwood Donuts. "Go on out and look at the fly fishing convention we're hosting. I swear, every one of those guys is standing around in their bucket caps with tackle sticking out of them. As if fishing lures makes a fashion statement anyway."

"Why are you so crabby about the fishermen out in the lobby?" Ruby Cobb asked him. She stood in her normal place in front of the prep table making side dishes for the daily boxed lunches. "You do know that we get a lot of money in our economy from folks like them, right?"

"I know that we have a fishing tournament at the lake every year that brings in a lot of money," Orson said. "But I don't know a thing about these weekend fishermen."

"Collectively, they bring in a nice sum to the local economy every year," Ruby said. "Since I've been on the city council, one of the things I've found most surprising is how much these small groups of folks actually help."

"So, what do you want me to do about it?" Orson mumbled.

"Maybe just behave yourself once in a while," Maggie said. She tied a clean apron around herself and patted Orson on his back. "How about you frost the cinnamon rolls and I'll take over the dining room for a little while?"

"Deal." Orson pulled a frosting spatula out of the drawer closest to him and swiped the bucket of icing from the counter. He cast an ornery smile in her direction and plopped himself down on an empty wooden stool in front of the baker's table.

Maggie sighed loudly and smiled. She loved the older man more than anything, but he could be cantankerous. The older he became, the more that fact became the truth. She pushed through the swinging door and smiled at the five men in angler hats, gathered around a table in the middle of the dining room.

She grabbed a fresh pot of coffee and made her way around the table with refills. "Does anyone need more cream? Sugar?"

"No, thank you," a couple of the fishermen said as she made her way around.

"Can I get you fellas anything else?" Maggie asked before she went back to the counter. A van pulled up in front of the donut shop. She counted several heads in the vehicle preparing to step out and come inside.

"Oh, ma'am, you might check over in the corner," one of the guys said. "Jack and Tom sequestered themselves over there to exchange their top secret trout secrets."

Maggie turned her head to the row of booths on the far side of the donut shop near the restrooms. She spotted two similarly dressed men hunched over the table. She smiled at them and headed over to where they sat. On her way, she glanced at the passengers from the van who were standing just outside the doors chatting.

"Can I refill your cups, gentlemen?"

"Oh, uh," one of them said. He raised his head up and gazed at her. "Can I help you?"

"Coffee," Maggie said. "Would you like a refill? Your friends over there suggested I check with you all, too."

"Our friends?"

"Yeah, the other fishermen, over there at that table," Maggie said. She turned her body halfway and gestured toward them.

"Oh, oh, yeah," he said. He raised his coffee mug up toward her. "Why don't you fill 'er right on up and we can get back to planning out trout fishing strategies."

She smiled and made the rounds. She topped off their cups, which were practically full already. "Can I get you anything else?" she asked.

"No, I think we're all good here," the man said.

Maggie nodded at him one more time and headed back to the counter to wait on the new group of customers that had found their way inside. She replaced the carafe on the burner and turned the switch on the second large coffee pot to start brewing fresh coffee.

"Good morning," she said to the group of five women. They were all dressed in khaki pants or shorts and short-sleeved shirts, hiking boots or tennis shoes, and hats of one sort or another. "What can I get for you?"

"I would like a cup of coffee for starters," the first woman approached the counter. She looked upward at the menu boards above Maggie. "And I'd like to try one of your apple cider donuts, please."

She pulled a small coin purse from the pocket of her cargo shorts and handed over a ten dollar bill. Like the rest of the women, she was somewhere north of fifty but south of seventy.

"I got this," Naomi Gardner said. She emerged from the kitchen just in time to help with the orders. Maggie smiled and nodded at the next woman in line. She was grateful that it was Naomi who had stepped forward to help her out. Of all of her employees, she had recently come to love working with Naomi the most. Ruby was an exception, of course, as her best friend and business partner they worked together like a well-oiled machine.

"How can I help you?" Maggie asked the next woman.

"Oh, I would like a latte and a glazed donut," the small woman said in an even smaller voice.

"Would you like a flavored latte?" Maggie asked her. "We have many to choose from." She pointed at the list on the menu behind her.

"Excuse me," a third woman stepped in front of the smaller one. She was the only one dressed in long pants. She crossed her arms over her bright purple shirt and glared at Maggie. "I want to know if you serve vegan donuts."

"I, well," Maggie stammered for a moment. She was shocked at the audacity of the woman to interrupt one of her companions ordering her breakfast.

"Well? It's not that difficult of a question to answer," the woman said.

Maggie caught her breath and sighed. She felt Naomi sidle up next to her. "It's not that it's a difficult question to answer," she said.

"Okay, then," the woman said a little too loudly. "What's the answer?"

Maggie felt Naomi's hand on her shoulder. "The answer is no, we do not serve vegan donuts," Maggie managed to say at last. "They are fried in vegetable shortening but contain egg and milk products."

"Then are those egg and milk products at least organic?" the woman asked. "Never mind, I suppose that might be too much to hope for in a backwater town like this."

"Okay, that's enough," Naomi said. "Why don't you step back and let your friend here finish ordering?"

"I beg your pardon?"

"Just step back, Talia," the last woman in line said. "Let Cissy order and wait your turn."

"Wait my turn? I have been waiting!" Talia turned completely around and faced the woman straight on.

Maggie looked past the women in front of her to the men seated at the table in the middle of the dining room. A couple of them stood and carried their coffee mugs across the room and over to the other two fishermen seated at the booth alone.

"I don't know about you, gentlemen," one of the men from the table said. "But this is turning into quite an entertaining morning!"

"Sit down, Stu," one of the other men said and clapped him hard on the back. Stu plopped down in the space across from the first two men and laughed.

"Ma'am," Maggie said to the smaller woman. "Was there a latte flavor you would like?"

"Yes, I would like French vanilla, please," Cissy said. "And may I please have my donut heated up a bit?"

"You've got it." Naomi beamed at her from the display case. She took a glazed donut and carried it to the microwave while Maggie entered the order.

"Okay, is it my turn now?" Talia asked loudly.

"No," Naomi said glibly. "I think you should let everyone else go first so we can handle your special requests."

"You're rude," Talia said to Naomi.

"Not as rude as you," Naomi replied.

"I would like to speak to the manager," Talia insisted. She crossed her arms.

"You're talking to the owner," Orson's voice boomed behind her.

"I am the owner," Maggie confirmed.

"It's okay," the woman behind Talia said with the wave of her hand. "I will gladly give my order to that fine silver fox behind you." She stepped over and stood straight across the counter from Orson.

"You are ridiculous, Susie," Talia said. She turned back to Maggie. "Where do you source your flour from?"

Maggie sighed. "From a commercial vendor," she said. "Just like almost everything else we use here. We do not have any vegan or organic options."

"How about your coffee? Is that organic at least?" she asked with a sneer.

"No, but it is fair trade," Maggie quipped. She almost pointed out the fact that of all of the things she had asked about, fair trade practices were not one of them.

"What she is trying to tell you, Princess Talia, is that if you want something more special, you're going to need to rent a car and drive into Joplin or all the way to Saint Louis for a specialty shop," the last woman in line said.

"Just give me a cup of coffee," Talia said at last. "I suppose you don't have fresh stevia leaves to soak in my cup, do you?"

"You suppose right, lady," Orson grumbled at the her as he tried to avoid Susie, who was still gawking at him from across the counter.

CHAPTER TWO

Maggie watched the group of women take their place at the front of the donut shop near the window.

Talia took the chair at the head of the table and spread napkins out in front of her, and then rested her arms on them.

Hannah returned to the counter for her order, a warm vanilla-blackberry scone, and motioned Maggie over to her. "I want to apologize for Talia," she said. "You'll notice that I did not use the term, 'friend.' She's a member of a bird watching group on the same trip we are on. And we all wound up at the bed and breakfast in town."

Maggie smiled and patted the woman on the hand. "Don't worry about it," she said. "Talia isn't the first person I've run into with a demanding way about her. You get used to it in this business."

"Have you always owned this place?" Hannah asked her.

Maggie shook her head. "My aunt owned this place long before I did, and she was open for many years. We even have a new location about a half hour west of here, run by my son."

"Wow," Hannah said with a genuine smile. "That is impressive! I just love the view around here. And that Dogwood House where we are all staying is just exquisite."

"That belonged to my aunt, too," Maggie smiled. "I spent many hours there growing up. And Gretchen LeClair, the current owner, has done amazing things starting with converting it to a bed and breakfast." She decided to skip over the fact the Gretchen was dating the man who Susie had been fawning over since she'd walked in.

Hannah nodded. "I agree fully with you," she said. She leaned over the counter and whispered. "I'll tell you what, if I can survive this group of ladies and these obnoxious fishermen over the next week, I will be back with my husband in the fall. Wait until he gets a load of this place! He was a baker in Seattle for many years, until we moved to Omaha. Anyway, I promise you he won't be harassing you for any vegan or organic donuts."

Maggie smiled and thanked the woman for her kindness.

"You know I can hear you, Hannah," Talia called from their table.

"We know everyone can hear you, lady," one of the fishermen shouted from the other side of the donut shop. "I think every trout in the entire county heard you."

"Nobody asked you for your opinion," Talia said. "I don't need a gaggle of smelly men determined to plunder the clear streams in these hills."

"Plunder? You aren't one of those crazy environmentalists, too, are you?" the man named Bob asked her.

"I guess we should have known that based on your request for vegan donuts!" His round face reddened from his exuberant laughter. The remaining men erupted into knee-slapping laughter. Talia left her seat at the table and rushed over to the other side of the dining room. She pushed into the middle of the group of men and raised her voice. Maggie watched the melee in disbelief. Soon another one of the women from the birdwatching group made her way across the room as well.

Hannah stood in front of the counter and rolled her eyes. "I think we're all a little old for a rumble at the donut shop, ladies," she called to the women now gathered across the room.

Every single one of them ignored her. They were gathered around the booths now, some standing, some still seated, with arms and voices raised debating the merits of everything from veganism to sustainable fishing to the philosophies of environmentalists. One of the men even mentioned the stupidity of venturing into the woods to observe birds. The insult against birdwatching brought all of the women except for Hannah around the table.

"I think we need to call Brooks at the police station to break this up," Orson leaned into Maggie and whispered. "And I think we need to do it soon." He nodded toward the group. Several smaller groups had formed, one or two fishermen squaring off with one of the women. A few of the men who had been seated stood up and others sat down in their place. Maggie had lost track of who had started out where.

Talia's group was the loudest by far. She stood at the end of a table and was surrounded by people. Two men were on their feet shouting at her. Her voice carried the same volume as the other people. Fingers pointed in faces and arms flew high over heads in exasperation. Maggie thought if eye-rolling was an Olympic sport, these older folks would give any teenage girl stiff competition. Voices bounced off of the walls and things were getting more hectic by the minute.

It was only when two members of the Dogwood Mountain Police Department pushed through the doors of the donut shop and approached the booth that some of the fishermen took a step back and disengaged from the shouting. Talia continued to stand toe to toe with the loudest member of the group. She was still shouting when Brooks Macklin himself took her by the arm and pulled her away from the table.

"Lady, I am going to arrest you for disorderly conduct if you don't quiet down now," he shouted over her.

"And who are you to tell me to be quiet?" Talia shot back.

"The chief of police for one," Brooks said. He pulled out a chair in the center of the room and sat her firmly down in it. "Officer Hastings here is going to sit right by you while I speak with the gentlemen on the other side of the room."

"Of course, you're going to take their side," Talia wailed. "Men stick together, am I right?"

"Officer Hastings is female, and she is not afraid

to put you in handcuffs and place you in the back of a police car if you don't cooperate," Brooks warned. "Sit there, be quiet, and let me get to the bottom of this." He returned to the other side of the dining room where the men were still cloistered around the booth. The group was suddenly hushed. They gathered close around the table, clustered together like football players in a huddle on the field. Brooks approached the group and placed his hand on one of the men's shoulders.

"What's happening over here?" he asked. The man looked up at him and stepped back from the table. Maggie was taken back by the odd look on the man's face. Just minutes before he had been loud-mouthed and sarcastic with one finger pointed in Talia's face. Only now his face had paled by several shades. His eyes were wide and disbelieving and his mouth gaped open. Brooks studied the man for a moment, and then turned his attention to the rest of the crowd. "Okay, everybody. Step back." He pulled another one of the men away from the table and stopped cold. One of the men seated at the table, the round-faced man named Bob, leaned over with his head down on the table. His arms were sprawled out around him and he was not moving.

"What's his name?" Brooks asked.

"Bob Jensen," one of the other men offered.

"Okay, Mr. Jensen, are you all right?" Brooks asked. He cleared the rest of the men away and moved into the seat next to the man. "Bob, are you okay, buddy?"

"Maybe he had a heart attack from all of the excitement," Talia jeered from her place next to Officer Hastings.

"Shut up, lady," another of the men said. "Hey, Bob!" He shook the man by the shoulder.

"Just stay back," Brooks said. He leaned over Bob and stiffened suddenly. He stood up and cast his eyes around the room. He locked eyes with Maggie and nodded in her direction. "Call Brett, now," he mouthed. He then took the radio off of his lapel and muttered something into the receiver to the dispatcher about sending an ambulance to Dogwood Donuts.

Another pair of officers arrived at the donut shop then. One by one they began walking the fishermen and the birdwatchers out of the donut shop until only Talia and the still unconscious Bob Jensen remained. Maggie dialed Brett's number and left a brief message on his voicemail that Brooks needed him at the donut shop. She was about to hang up the phone when Brooks pulled the man's head back. She gasped and dropped her phone when she saw him. His face was white, but his neck was purple and blue. She narrowed her eyes to understand what was there, stuck in the side of his neck just above his collar. Light reflected off of the metal object buried deep in his flesh.

"What is that?" Naomi asked from where she stood frozen behind the counter. "Is it alive?"

CHAPTER THREE

Sheriff Brett Mission arrived at the donut shop ten minutes after Maggie had called and left her message to him. He walked straight into the donut shop and headed right for the chief. Not too long ago, Brett himself had been the chief of police and Brooks Macklin had been his main officer. A retiring county sheriff and an uncontested election had shifted things around, and both men were happy about the change.

"The sheriff is now in charge of this investigation," Brooks announced to Officer Hastings and the others who had come to assist in crowd control. Hastings herself was new to the force. Maggie had only seen her in passing.

Brooks and Brett bent their heads together in

conversation. Maggie headed back to the kitchen. Orson followed quickly after her. "Are you alright?" he asked her.

Maggie leaned against one of the large metal sinks and shook her head. "I just need to catch my breath for a second," she said.

"I can't believe that just happened," Naomi said.

"Why don't you just come on back here and catch your breath, too," Orson said. He ducked into the store room and returned with two wooden stools.

"I think we ought to shut down for the time being," Ruby announced when she emerged from the cooler. "I just put everything back in there for now."

"Did Brooks or Brett ask us to close down?" Naomi asked.

"I don't think we should wait," Maggie said. She pushed off of the sink and headed back through the swinging door to the other side. She walked across the front of the counter until she was close to the other side where the police were still gathered. She averted her eyes from the body that was slumped over the table. From the snippets of conversations Maggie gathered that the medical examiner was on his way.

"Brett," Maggie said quietly. "I mean, Sheriff Mission."

Brett turned his attention to her and stepped

around the end of the counter. "How are you holding up?" he asked.

"You sound like Orson," she said. "I was just coming out here to tell you that we're going to shut the donut shop down for the rest of the day and for as long as you need it."

"Thank you. I think we have just about chased everyone else off that wasn't a witness and I've got the rest of the folks outside talking to the deputies now," Brett said. "Why don't you all do what you need to do to close up shop in the back and I will pull each of you one at a time to take your statements. I don't want any of you out here at all." He looked at her. "And that starts with you."

"Right, of course. We're about done putting everything away and we can do the statements in my office if you want. That way no one is out here, but you can still get what you need from us." Maggie felt a chill climb up her spine. The fact that a murder had taken place right in front of her eyes without her even knowing it hadn't quite come home to her just yet.

"Yeah," Brett said. "I just need to find out what everyone saw."

"Okay. Who would you like to start with?" Maggie asked.

"Why don't you go first? I'll be back there in a minute."

"Okay," she agreed, heading back toward the kitchen to tell everyone what Brett had said.

A few minutes later, Brett joined her in the office. He took a seat across from her and began right away. "Where were you standing when all of this happened?"

"Behind the counter right in front of the iPad. I was taking the orders of the women who had come inside from the van. I was waiting on the second woman, a little thing, when the third woman in line stepped in front of her and interrupted everything to ask if I served vegan donuts," Maggie said.

"And then what happened?"

"When I tried to explain to her that the donuts were made with milk and egg products she interrupted again and asked if the ingredients were at least organic," Maggie said.

Brett chuckled slightly. "Did she sit down then?"

"No, Naomi stepped forward and told her to wait her turn," Maggie said.

"Did she?"

"Not really. She got a little more belligerent," Maggie said. "I was trying to finish the lady's order, but the other woman ran her mouth more and some of the men in the middle of the room started weighing in on the matter."

"So, the men were not all together at first?" Brett asked.

Maggie shook her head. "No, there were about five of them in the middle of the dining room at first. In fact, they were sort of giving the other two sitting over on the other side where the murder took place a hard time about sitting over there all alone," she said.

"Were the other two men joining in on the discussion at that point?" he asked.

"No, they were sort of huddled around and discussing something pretty quietly," she said. "But when everything started to get out of hand between Talia and everyone else, the five who were seated in the middle moved over to the booth area to join the other two."

"Where was Bob Jensen originally?"

"At the table in the middle of the dining room," Maggie said.

"And do you know when he ended up seated in the booth?"

Maggie closed her eyes she tried to replay the scene in her mind. "I don't remember seeing that happen, at all," she said. "The next thing I knew, the men were over there, the women were at their table, and we called the cops."

"And that's when Brooks discovered the man was dead," Brett said.

"That's when he discovered the man was dead, yes," Maggie said.

"I have one more question for you," Brett said. "When you were waiting on any of the men, did you happen to see a lure like the one that was buried in his neck?" He passed his phone to her with a photo of the lure on the screen.

Maggie studied the screen and shut her eyes. "They were all wearing that kind of hat that had hooks and lures all over them. But I don't remember seeing the lure you are showing me. I admit that I wasn't really looking, though."

"Okay," Brett said. He smiled at her. "I'm going to have some of the deputies speak with everyone else so you guys can get out of here as fast as you can."

"You know where the extra keys are in the office," Maggie said. She stood up from her desk and thought about how badly she wanted to overhear what Talia was saying to whoever was questioning her. The last time she'd seen her, her arms were folded, making her seem as unapproachable as ever, but it was the self-satisfied grin on her face that sent Maggie over the edge. It was almost as if she was unaware that she was sitting in the middle of a crime scene.

CHAPTER FOUR

"I would love to have extra help tomorrow, Mom," Bradley said to her an hour after she left work. It was just past noon, and she could hear the activity in the background. "I really need to hire two more people. If Naomi or Myra or even you or Ruby want to stop by and help out, I am all for it."

"Not Orson?"

"No way," Bradley said.

"Why not?"

"Because when that old man is around me, all I want to do is sit down with him and pour a tumbler of whiskey and listen to him talk about the past," Bradley said. "I don't get a thing done when he is around."

"Okay." Maggie laughed. "I understand that

completely. I'll let the others know what you said about coming in tomorrow and possibly the next day, but I will likely not be there tomorrow."

"Where are you going to be?"

"I have a bunch of food to deal with before it goes bad," Maggie said. "Depending on whether I get Brett's blessing or not, I plan to take that food up to the Dogwood House so that it doesn't go to waste."

"Isn't that where all of the people who were at the donut shop today are staying?" he asked her. "The birdwatchers and the fishermen?"

"It is," Maggie said. "But there really isn't any place else where I can take day-old donuts and boxed lunches. And besides, Gretchen is going to have her hands full with all of them stuck there until they are given the okay to leave. I'll admit, too, that I'm feeling guilty because we can't do our normal break-fast and lunch deliveries until further notice."

"Are you sure it doesn't have anything to do with you wanting to get a chance to talk to each of them individually?"

"Not especially," Maggie said. "I was there when it happened, remember? I'm not sure if there's anything else I can find out that I don't already know."

"But you'll be sure to find that out one way or the other." Her son chuckled. "Just be careful, Mom."

"I promise that I will not be reckless with my safety when I deliver yesterday's donuts to the folks at the Dogwood House," Maggie said. She hung up the phone and texted Brett to let him know that she planned to stop by early in the morning in order to take the remaining donuts to the bed and breakfast.

Brett texted her back and let her know that she could have access to the kitchen, but that they would still be in the dining area processing it for evidence for a little while longer. She waited for an admonition from him to stay away from some of the house guests, but it never came.

Maggie decided not to delay her delivery to the bed and breakfast. As strange as it felt to walk back inside the kitchen knowing that a murder had taken place on the other side of the building just a few hours before, Maggie was happy that she could take the left-over donuts to the Dogwood House where they would not go to waste.

She let herself in the kitchen through the back door. She could hear someone on the other side and decided to poke her head through the swinging door to announce herself. She pushed the door open and was surprised to see Officer Hastings there alone on the other side of the yellow tape that had been strewn around the booth area.

"Hi, hello," Maggie said quickly. "I spoke with Sheriff Mission, and he told me that I could have access to the kitchen to pick something up."

"Alright," Officer Hastings said. "I think he said the same thing to the chief."

"Okay, well, I just wanted to let you know that I'll be back here for a half an hour or so. I am going to box up the leftover donuts and the lunches that are in the cooler to take them to the bed and breakfast," Maggie said.

"Have at it," the officer said. Her eyes shifted to the empty display case. Maggie smiled and then turned back to the kitchen.

She thought about the young woman's behavior as she searched for extra donut boxes in the store room. She found the boxes on the top shelf above the coffee cups and pulled them down off of the shelf.

Why had the officer been so abrupt? Was there some new evidence that had been discovered? Or maybe she was just uncomfortable being there at the same time she was there. Either way, Maggie fought the urge to go back out into the dining room to ask her more questions. Instead, she made her way into the cooler to count the trays of donuts that remained.

"Ms. Sharpe?" Maggie heard a voice calling to her from the other side of the cooler door. "Are you still here?"

Maggie pushed the door back open and held it for a second. Officer Hastings stood in the middle of the kitchen. "I'm just in here getting things together," she said. "What's up?"

"I, well, I wanted to let you know something," she said. "I don't want you to be upset, but I really didn't think about it when I did it."

Maggie stepped out of the cooler and pushed the door shut behind her. "I'm sorry, what are you talking about?"

Officer Hastings took her hat off and stared at the floor. "I hope that you don't feel the need to report this to the chief, but if you do, I will understand," she said. "But I helped myself to one of the donuts in the cooler."

"You ate one of the donuts?"

Officer Hastings shook her head. "Actually, I had two," she said. "I honestly wasn't trying to steal, but the chief left me here to watch over things until they could come back with more equipment to process the scene. I think he and the sheriff were worried about one of the fishermen or the birdwatchers coming back here for whatever reason."

"How long have you been here?"

"Since this morning."

"Officer Hastings, what is your first name?"

"It's Kacy."

"Kacy, would you like a proper lunch? We have these boxed lunches here and I'm going to be taking them to the bed and breakfast as well," Maggie said.

"You aren't mad?"

"I would be more upset if you just sat here and starved instead," Maggie said. "Is there an officer at the bed and breakfast as well?"

Officer Hastings shook her head. "I think they're only doing occasional check ins," she said. "The sheriff and the chief both told the fishermen and the women who were here this morning not to leave town until we can rule out them as suspects."

Maggie opened the door to the cooler and pulled two boxed lunches off of the shelves. "I'm going to leave both of these here for you," she said. "I'll talk to Gretchen first, but why don't you let the chief know that whoever is watching over Dogwood House can stop by and get some food too?"

"Are you really not angry with me for helping myself to the donuts?"

"No, I am not," Maggie said with a smile. "How long have you been with the force?"

"Less than a month," she said.

"Okay, well, you are going to find out very soon that the police department and the donut shop have a pretty close relationship," she said. "Same with the sheriff's department."

"I know the chief is married to one of your employees," Officer Hastings said.

"The chief and his wife opened their home to another one of our employees, who is now a grandpa to their baby," Maggie said. "And my son runs our sister location in Hunter Springs. The chief and his wife have watched my grandson, too."

"And you and the sheriff are in love." Kacy Hastings laughed. Maggie felt her face fall. "Oh, I am so sorry! I didn't mean to get so personal."

Maggie forced herself to smile and shook her head. "The sheriff and I are dating and in love," she said. "Anyway, you get the picture. The donut shop and local law enforcement are quite entwined. If you are here, help yourself. No harm done."

"Thank you, Ms. Sharpe."

"Please call me Maggie. Now, if you don't have anything else to do, how about helping me out to my car with these donut boxes?"

Kacy smiled. "Let me just take a quick peek back out front and make sure that everything is okay," she said. "And then I'll be right back here to help."

Maggie stacked the boxes on the baker's table while she waited for Kacy to return. She took a tray from the drying rack and began to fill it with the boxed lunches.

"Do you know how to make yourself some coffee?" Maggie asked a minute later.

"I don't know how to make a new pot of coffee," Kacy admitted. "Those machines out there are much too fancy for me."

"Well, while you're back here, take a look in the cooler and find the milk and juices I have available," Maggie said. "And all you have to do to brew a new pot of coffee is turn the machine on. They are all preloaded with coffee grounds and water. And the syrups and creamers are all in the stainless steel refrigerator out there behind the counter. If you are here, help yourself, got it?"

"Yes, ma'am," Kacy said with a smile. She picked up a stack of donut boxes and followed Maggie out to her car.

CHAPTER FIVE

Maggie thanked Kacy once again and reassured her
that she was welcome to use anything she might need
while she was still at the donut shop watching over
the crime scene.

She wondered what Brett or Brooks might be up
to. Her back seat was filled to the brim with the day's
pastries and boxed lunches. Gretchen was aware that
she was coming to deliver the goodies, but Maggie
had not told her exactly when she would be there.

Maggie drove up the familiar hill to the large
estate house and pulled into the driveway. She drove
off to the side out of the way of the vehicles that were
already parked, including a car from the Dogwood
Mountain Police Department. She recognized the

chief's car and wondered if Brooks alone was inside conducting further interviews.

"Oh, you are right on time," Gretchen called out to her from the large porch. "I was just trying to figure out what to make for these people. I swear that they are like caged animals right now."

"Well, I have boxed lunches and leftover donuts and pastries with me," Maggie said. "Although I am ashamed to say that I am unsure exactly what Ruby made for the lunches today."

"Oh, I just hope some of her famous apple slaw is in there," Gretchen said. Her silver hair shimmered next to her silver hoop earrings. Maggie had noted the difference in her appearance in the past several months and wondered what Orson thought of it or if it was due to their relationship.

"I suppose we shall soon see what is in there," Maggie said. She climbed the steps to the porch and followed Gretchen into the familiar kitchen. Gretchen's groundskeeper Albert appeared and helped carry in the rest of the trays.

"The chief is in the main foyer speaking with someone right now," Gretchen said quietly. "I don't know who he is interviewing, but he's been here since earlier this morning. I just can't believe that one of my guests was murdered."

"I can't believe someone was murdered inside my donut shop this morning," Maggie said ruefully.

"Oh, yes." Gretchen turned toward her. She placed her hand on Maggie's shoulder. "Listen to me going on and on about having one of my guests killed and you were right there when it happened. And now your business is closed down for the foreseeable future. Are you handling all of this okay?" She pulled a chair out from the small round table in the kitchen and practically pushed Maggie down in it.

"Oh, don't worry about me, Gretchen," Maggie said. "I'm doing alright, even if I am a little bit freaked out."

"What about the rest of the crew? I haven't had a chance to speak with Orson today," Gretchen said. She took the seat across from Maggie. The fact that she'd mentioned Orson made Maggie smile.

"Well, Bradley said the rest of the crew is welcome to help him out in Hunter Springs over the next couple of days," Maggie said. "Although he specifically requested that Orson not be among them."

"Oh," Gretchen said. Her face twisted into a frown. "Orson adores Bradley. And he told me himself that he considers himself the grandfather of two children, Wyatt and Lexi."

"Oh, my son adores him as well! That's exactly why he doesn't want him to come there to work," Maggie said. She covered the older woman's hand with her own. "He's afraid he won't get anything done all day because all he will want to do is sit around and talk to Orson."

"Oh! That makes me feel so much better," Gretchen said. "You have no idea what it does for that old man to be so beloved."

"You have no idea what that old man does for the rest of us," Maggie said. She noted the color rising in the older woman's cheeks.

"Well, let's take a look at these lunch boxes, shall we?"

Maggie nodded and rose from her chair. She picked up one of the plain brown boxes and set it on the counter next to the old fashioned stove. Gretchen followed suit. "Oh, my," she said and pulled a small container of apple slaw out of the box. "Ruby is just so creative! Look at this! Apple slaw, apple cider donut, spinach and strawberry salad, and fancy chicken salad sandwiches! Are these croissants home-made by you?"

"No," Maggie said sheepishly. "I'm afraid those are bought."

"I don't know how you would have the time to

make croissants as well as all of the other things you make every morning," Gretchen whispered. "Look at these gourmet sandwiches. I see grapes, walnuts, candied cranberries."

"These are my favorite sandwiches," Maggie said. "Why don't we get these set out for your guests? Let's hold some back for the chief and whoever else is on patrol here."

"You read my mind." Gretchen smiled. She set several serving trays out. One at a time, they disassembled the boxed lunches and filled up two glasses with ice per tray. Maggie helped her assemble several large glass decanters of lemonade and sweet tea for the tables. They carried the trays and the decanters to the large dining space set up between the kitchen and the living room. Gretchen had done away with a single, large dining room table and replaced it instead with a dozen two-person bistro sets.

"Just set a tray down at each chair," Gretchen instructed Maggie. They filled the tables with the lunch trays and returned for the glasses.

"Fancy seeing you here," Hannah said when she saw her. Several of the other women followed her into the room.

"I thought you worked at the donut shop," Talia said. She sneered in Maggie's direction.

"Maggie owns the donut shop, and her aunt owned this house when she was growing up, Ms. Henderson," Gretchen told the woman.

"Well, why is she here now?"

"Looks like she brought us something to eat," Hannah said. "As far as I am concerned, Maggie is my new favorite resident of this charming little town."

"You wouldn't consider this town quite as charming if your best friend had just been murdered in it." Maggie looked up. One of the men from the fishing party walked into the dining room.

"I am so sorry about your friend," she said.

"You didn't do it," he said and slumped down in one of the chairs. Maggie thought he indeed did look like he had just lost his best friend.

"How are you holding up, Joe?" Gretchen asked the man. She turned to Maggie. "Have you met Mr. Lowman?"

"We spoke at the donut shop, although I wasn't clear on his name," she said. "How are you, Mr. Lowman?"

"It's Joe, and I am about as well as can be expected under the circumstances," he said.

"We would all like for this to be over and done with so we can go back home," another of the men said. Maggie recognized him as one of the quieter men who had been in the booth earlier that morning.

"Jack, you are welcome to sit down and have a meal," Gretchen said. "You and your friends need to eat."

"Thank you, ma'am," Jack said. "I'll go tell the guys and see what they have to say."

"Who's with the police chief right now?" Joe asked.

"Cissy Baumgartner," Hannah offered. "She's the little bitty lady Talia here likes to interrupt."

"Why don't you just lay off, Hannah?" Talia snapped. She walked around the tables and poked through the trays of food.

"Why don't you keep your meat hooks off of other people's food?" The voice of another one of the fishermen boomed through the house. Maggie recognized him as one of the men who had been seated close to Bob Jensen at the table. She wondered if he was another close friend of the deceased man, like Joe Lowman appeared to be.

"Ian Roberts, Maggie Sharpe," Gretchen introduced them. Ian Roberts looked like the kind of man who would have been right at home with a fishing pole and a bucket of minnows. He stood over six feet, and like the man who had been killed earlier that morning, appeared to like eating fish as much as he did catching it. He wore a button down shirt tucked into khaki pants. His gut protruded over his pants, just as Bob Jensen's had.

"It's a pleasure, Mr. Roberts," Maggie said. "Were you close to Mr. Jensen as well?"

"Just call me Ian," he said. "And no, I just met him on this fishing trip."

"So, you all don't know each other already?" Maggie asked. She had taken it for granted that they were all close friends on a fishing trip together."

"Not all of us," Jack explained. "Most of us met on a website dedicated to setting up these excursions in different places across the country. I think Joe and Bob knew each other, of course."

"I thought you and your two companions were friends," Joe said to Jack. Maggie recognized the two other men who had just walked into the room as the same men who had been seated at the booth far away from the rest of the fishermen at the donut shop.

"I was just coming to see if you guys wanted something to eat," Jack said to them.

"I thought I smelled good food," one of Jack's quieter companions said. If she could separate the men by where they had been seated that morning, she would guess that the men seated at the table along with Bob and Joe would have been construction workers or cowboys or country lawyers. The other three including Jack Wesley looked like they had just flown in from a convention of accountants and tax attorneys.

"I'm shocked that you can smell anything above your own stink," Talia said.

"Excuse me," Jack Wesley said. "What is your problem?"

"Perhaps you ought to take your lunch out on the porch or back to your room, Ms. Henderson," Gretchen suggested.

"Why don't you make these murderers eat their lunch in their cells, Madam Warden?" Talia snapped.

"Who are you calling murderers?" All five of the men in the room stood up and faced her.

"I think we all need to just calm down and have a seat," Maggie said. She stood in the middle of the room with her hands raised in front of her.

"I know every one of you is a murderer," Talia said. She walked in a circle and gestured toward the men.

"That's the only reason any of you are here. Look at yourselves! You wear your weapons of slaughter on your clothing, for Pete's sake!"

"Ma'am," Brooks said from the doorway of the

dining room. "I'm going to need you to calm down and have a seat right now." He made no bones about his anger toward her.

"Why? Are you going to protect the killers, Officer?" Talia sneered at him.

"I am here to find out who the killer is," Brooks shouted.

Talia scowled at him. "I am not talking about whoever killed that awful man from earlier today! As far as I'm concerned, that is one less murderer on this planet," she hollered. "I am talking about the helpless creatures in those streams and lakes that these monsters pillage every time they step into their little costumes and cast a line into the water!"

A hush fell over the room. Joe stood up from his seat and threw his napkin on the food tray. He walked around the small table and stood in the middle of the room and stopped just a few feet from Talia. The willowy woman squared her shoulders and smirked as he approached.

"Lady, a man died this morning," he said. "And the fact that you want to celebrate that and are worried more about a few sad creatures that were put on this planet for the use of man and other animals higher up in the food chain makes me wonder just what kind of a person you really are."

"Easy now," Brooks said from the doorway.

"I am just the sort of person who knows that not all creatures on this planet were created equal," Talia said with a huff.

Maggie fully expected her to turn on her heel and head back to whichever room in the bed and breakfast she had rented. Instead, she plopped herself down at one of the tables in front of one of the food trays and began separating the vegetarian offerings from the meat sandwich, which she handled like a dead skunk and tossed in the middle of the table.

CHAPTER SIX

Maggie drove out of town to Ruby's farm as the sun dipped in the sky. She was still flustered by the experience earlier in the day at the Dogwood House. A text from Brett told her that he and a couple of deputies had arrived just after she had left in order to assist the Dogwood Mountain Police Department with the multiple interviews that would be required to help them weed through potential suspects.

When she arrived at Ruby's, her mind was spinning with the words she heard coming out of Talia Henderson's mouth.

"That woman is doing a pretty good job of making herself look like she is the perfect suspect," she told Ruby when she walked through the back of her best friend's old farm house.

"Did she really call all of them murderers?"

Maggie nodded. "She said that, and she told them that Bob's death merely meant that there was one less murderer in the world," Maggie said. "She considers fishing murder."

"This is the Ozarks," Ruby said. "I wonder what she would think about the hunting that goes on around here."

"I can only imagine," Maggie said. She looked around Ruby's large kitchen for the first time since she arrived. Mixing bowls, pans, and trays were scattered all over her counters. "What on earth are you up to in here?"

Ruby grinned and headed for the countertop deep fryer she had next to her large stove. She pulled up the basket and used a pair of tongs to remove three donuts. She set them on a plate and rolled them in simple cinnamon and sugar. She set one of the donuts on a plate and handed it to Maggie. "Try this," she said.

"I've had donuts before, Ruby," she joked and picked up the donut. She studied for a moment. It looked and smelled like any other donut they had at either one of their locations. She shrugged her shoulders and took a bite. The taste was just slightly different. "What is this?"

"Do you like it?" Ruby asked her. "How does it taste?"

"It tastes like a cinnamon sugar donut," Maggie said, and took a second bite. "But there is something that is ever so slightly different."

"Different good or different bad?"

"Just different," Maggie said. "It's not as rich, maybe. But it's good. Are you going to tell me what I just put into my mouth?"

Ruby smiled. "You just ate a vegan donut," she said. "And I am not at all surprised that you think it isn't as rich. Vegan butter just isn't the same as real butter."

"When did you decide to try this?" Maggie asked. "Please don't tell me that awful woman made you do this."

Ruby shook her head. She picked up a donut for herself and took a big bite. "Her words made me curious," she said. "I certainly didn't make these for her benefit, but it did make me think about expanding the menu just a little bit."

"You have definitely made vegan taste better than I ever thought it could," Maggie said. "What are those?" She pointed to a cookie sheet with another half dozen donuts on it.

"Those are an experiment gone wrong," Ruby

said. "Try one at your own risk."

Maggie eyed the pan. She picked up one of the donuts and pinched off a piece and popped it into her mouth.

"Oh, that's terrible," she said. Ruby was prepared with a napkin. Maggie took the napkin from her and spit the bite out. "That's just awful! What on earth is this?"

Ruby held out a small trash can and waited while Maggie tossed the napkin and the rest of the donut in it. "That is the reason that neither Dogwood Mountain Donuts nor Hunter Springs Donuts will ever serve gluten free anything."

"Those were gluten free?"

Ruby nodded. "I tried four different recipes and that was the best out of the four," she said. "But I could not get away from the chemical taste."

"Yes! That's what I was tasting! Something weird and not natural at all," Maggie said.

"This is the one time in my entire life that those words are not insulting to me at all," Ruby laughed. "I think I am a fairly accomplished chef and there was nothing I could do to make those taste right. I have no doubt there are professionals who have cracked the code, but I have not. And I don't think I am going to try any longer, either."

Maggie chuckled and took a seat at the counter. "What smells like cinnamon rolls?" she asked.

"Vegan cinnamon rolls," Ruby said. "I decided to try a batch of them, but these I baked." She picked up a set of pot holders and opened the oven, pulled out a tray of perfectly baked cinnamon rolls, and set them on top of the stove. "I have not tried this vegan frosting on them yet." She moved to the fridge and pulled out a bowl of prepared icing.

"How do you make vegan icing?"

"This is actually vegan buttercream frosting," Ruby said. "And I'm not sure how it's going to turn out." She smeared a bit of frosting on half of one of the cinnamon rolls and passed it to Maggie. "Try it with and without the frosting."

Maggie first took a generous bite of the unfrosted portion of the roll. "It's soft and very cinnamony," she said. "I can't taste too much of a difference, although it is a lot like the donut. Not as rich as I'm used to."

"Okay, and with the frosting?"

Maggie turned the donut around and took a generous bite of the frosted cinnamon roll. "Hmmm," she said. "I am not sure about this."

"What do you mean?" Ruby asked her. She held another cinnamon roll and smeared frosting over it.

"It's sweet when you first take a bite of it,"

Maggie explained. "But after a second, the frosting sort of leaves a weird feeling in your mouth. It's still very sweet, but there is an aftertaste."

Ruby nodded and took a large bite herself. She chewed for a second, then made a face. "Oh, you're right," she said. "It's like a greasy, filmy aftertaste." She turned around and carefully ridded herself of the bite.

"I like the vegan donuts themselves," Maggie said.

"I think we can safely offer a new variety of vegan donuts on the menu, but that's going to be about it," Ruby said. "I don't know about you, but I am not too interested in spending a lot of time making this frosting taste better. In fact, I'm really not sure what else I can do to make this better."

Maggie reached for another unfrosted cinnamon roll. "Maybe we can do a vegan cinnamon roll donut," she suggested. "Without any frosting on it, of course."

"That's actually not a bad idea," Ruby agreed. "I wonder what Miss Talia would think of these? Maybe I can take one of them with me when I stop by the Dogwood House in the morning."

"You're going to the bed and breakfast in the morning?" Maggie asked her.

"I promised Gretchen that I'd come in early and prepare a big breakfast for her guests," Ruby said. "Apparently, Brett told everyone that they still weren't allowed to leave just yet."

"Do you want an assistant?"

Ruby's face brightened. "I would love an assistant," she said. "In fact, do you think you could go by and get some of the coffee syrups from the donut shop? We could at least offer some limited coffee choices."

"I'll text Brett and make sure it's okay to go by," Maggie said. "But I'll be there first thing in the morning either way."

Maggie met Brett at the donut shop on her way home from Ruby's. He stood by and waited while she retrieved the flavored syrups and several varieties of creamers from behind the counter. "I have to be able to say that we preserved the crime scene at all times," he explained to her while he stood there.

"How much longer do you expect that this will be a crime scene?" Maggie asked him. "I mean, we can stand to be closed down for a day or two if we need to be, but what is there really here to investigate? I'm not a police officer, but I don't even see any physical evidence. It seems like all of the evidence you had left when the coroner left here with Bob's body."

Brett nodded. He walked her back through the kitchen and helped her load the bottles of syrups and creamer into her car. "There really isn't much," he said. "That's the very reason why we are taking so long to process it all."

"I don't think I get what you mean," Maggie said.

"I mean, we have very little to go on, so we want to take our time to make sure that we process the scene as thoroughly as we can," he said. "I am looking for absolutely anything, even if it is the smallest, most microscopic piece of evidence. We can't afford to miss anything."

"What happened during the interviews at the Dogwood House today?" Maggie asked him. "Did Brooks come up with anything?"

Brett shook his head. "Brooks interviewed everyone himself, and I followed up as well," he said. "We had one of my deputies double check things with a few of them, too."

"What do you mean by that, double checking a few things?" Maggie asked.

"We asked one of the deputies to double check a couple of facts, just to see if we could catch someone telling him something different," he explained. "Inconsistency is a big red flag."

"And what happened?"

"What happened is absolutely nothing," Brett said. He shut the car door and gazed up at the dark sky overhead. "We were fishing, Maggie. There is nothing so far that we have been able to grab onto with this case. No angle to go on. Not one of these people has given me even a thought of suspicion. I am truly at a loss."

"What about Talia? She seems quite outspoken about her hatred for the fishermen," Maggie said. "Do you think she might have killed Bob?"

"Was she anywhere near him the entire time they were shouting back and forth?" Brett asked her.

Maggie thought for a moment. She ran the images of the morning through her mind once more, then slowly shook her head. "No, she was never anywhere near him," she said. "The only people that were close to him were his fishing buddies."

"Right, which is why we have asked for the women to stay indoors while we continue to investigate," he said. "The suspect is going to be among the men, I am afraid."

"Unless Talia or one of the other women is more conniving and capable of crafty subterfuge than we are giving her credit for," Maggie said.

"Yeah, unless," Brett agreed.

CHAPTER SEVEN

Maggie slept fitfully overnight, dreaming of large-mouthed fish hooked on giant lures coming after her in the water. Twice she'd sat straight up in bed, covered in sweat and dreaming about monster fish chasing after her. She padded down the hallway and checked the empty guest room, still not used to the fact that her son and grandson were safely nestled in a house of their own thirty minutes away.

Tonight, she wished for a full house again.

She ran a glass of water from the tap and took a few sips to help wash away any remaining dreams. When she woke up the second time it was just under forty minutes before her alarm was set to go off anyway. She decided to stay up and enjoy a cup of her own coffee flavored by the cinnamon syrup from the donut shop.

Josie, Naomi, and Myra had decided to drive to Hunter Springs to help out there for the day. Myra drove separately in case Lexi's nanny needed for her to rush back home. Ruby informed Maggie that she would arrive at the Dogwood House a little before seven to begin preparing breakfast and had asked Maggie to be there around the same time.

It felt a bit like luxury, waiting so long to leave the house and taking her time with a cup of coffee in her own kitchen. She thought about rearranging the schedule to have an early morning or two off each week. Naomi had risen so quickly in her abilities that she could practically open the place up by herself and Myra could easily do the same, but with Lexi still so small, she had decided to take a step back from her ambitions to someday manage the donut shop on her own.

Maggie decided that she would bring up the subject of handing over more responsibility to Naomi to Ruby later on in the day. She figured both of them could use a morning off each week. In fact, Ruby had another cookbook contract to consider. Perhaps she would enjoy more time off as well. Maggie decided that if she could carve out more time away, she might even travel to Hunter Springs one day each week to help Bradley out until he was able to hire more help.

Just before seven, she loaded everything up in her car and headed across town to the Dogwood House for the second time in two days. Ruby's truck was already parked in the back of the house near the large shed. Maggie carried the syrups and creamers inside in a large box. She could hear the cooking sounds as she walked up the steps to the porch.

"Good morning," she said when she stepped inside the back door. "Where is everyone?"

"Still asleep, I guess," Ruby said. She stood at the large counter in the middle of the kitchen cutting up onions and mushrooms. "I've seen Gretchen and Albert once each. Gretchen was not dressed quite yet so I think she's in the shower now."

"None of the guests are up yet?" Maggie asked.

Ruby shook her head. "Not that I have seen, no," she said. "But that young girl, Officer Hastings is her name, has been here since before I arrived."

"Kacy is her first name," Maggie said. "She is a nice girl."

"She seems to be," Ruby said. She studied her best friend for a moment.

"What?" Maggie asked her.

"Oh, nothing," Ruby said with a grin. "I was just

trying to size up whether or not you were plotting some matchmaking."

"Matchmaking?"

"The pretty young police officer and your son." Ruby's grin broadened.

Maggie shook her head. "Oh, no," she said. "I'm not about to go down that road."

"Okay, just checking," Ruby whispered as Officer Hastings suddenly appeared in the kitchen.

"Good morning, Maggie," she said. She looked around the room.

"Did you lose something?" Maggie placed the creamers in the large kitchen refrigerator.

"I can't seem to find a couple of the male guests," the officer said. "Everyone was given explicit orders not to leave the bed and breakfast."

"Maybe they're still asleep," Ruby suggested. "Since they can't get up at the crack of dawn to go fishing, perhaps they decided just to sleep in."

"That's possible," Officer Hastings said. "But if I don't come across them in the next half hour, I'm going to run out of the benefit of the doubt to give them."

"They could be in the shower, too," Maggie added. Officer Hastings nodded and headed outside.

Maggie turned to Ruby and shrugged. "I guess we'll figure it out."

"One way or the other," Ruby said. "Now, how about you get into the cooler over there by the door and grab the blueberries and lemons."

"Lemons and blueberries? What am I making?" Maggie opened the cooler lid and pulled out a large bag of lemons and several small baskets of fresh blueberries.

"You're making lemon ricotta pancakes with a blueberry compote," Ruby said. "I've got the rest."

"Just tell me what I need to do, and I'll get started," Maggie said.

Ruby directed her to wash the blueberries in the sink. She filled a large pan with a small bit of water and set it on the large stove. Ruby remarked on the professional sized stove in the kitchen. Maggie quickly understood her appreciation for it. She turned on a low flame under the pan and set the blueberries carefully in the water.

Next she searched for a grater and followed Ruby's instructions with the lemons. She grated the zest off of several lemons and then sliced them open and pressed the juice out of them and into a quart-sized glass measuring cup. She set the lemon juice to the side for later and checked on the blueberries.

Meanwhile, Ruby busied herself across the kitchen. She grated potatoes with her own grater and pressed them between thick paper towels. She placed a large, heavy skillet on the stove and poured vegetables in it and turned the flame on medium below it. While the oil heated up, Ruby laid several strips of bacon on two large metal baking sheets and placed them in the oven. She set a second skillet on the stove and placed sausage links in it, and then covered the rest of the stove with a third pan, a cast iron skillet for the ham steaks. She turned her attention back to the potatoes and placed them in the sizzling oil.

"Thank goodness I had the sense to make my hollandaise sauce earlier this morning when I was still at home," she said. "Oh, and I also have a raspberry chutney for the ham."

"Are we serving any eggs?" Maggie asked her. She measured the flour into a large bowl for her pancakes.

Ruby nodded. "I'm making the omelets last," she said. "That's why I was cutting up the veggies when you came in."

Gretchen appeared in the kitchen just then, fully dressed and as fresh as a daisy. "What can I do to help?" she asked when she breezed past them.

"Make coffee," Maggie and Ruby said at the same

time. They laughed and turned back to their individual tasks.

"I thought I smelled the cooking of dead carcasses in here," Talia said when she appeared in the kitchen.

"Give it a rest today, Miss Henderson," Gretchen said from her palace by the sink. Maggie shot a look of shock at Ruby. Rarely did Gretchen ever utter a cross word to anyone.

Talia frowned but said nothing more. She folded her arms, much like a petulant child, and slid into one of the chairs that rested against the kitchen wall. "It would be nice if we could all just pack up and go home," she mumbled. "This vacation has been ruined anyway."

"You aren't planning to get out into the woods when the sheriff gives you guys the go-ahead?" Ruby asked her.

"If there's any time," Talia said.

"Do you have a job back home?" Maggie asked. "By the way, where do you live?"

"I'm from St. Joseph," Talia said.

"Missouri?" Gretchen asked her. "So, you aren't that far from home."

"Not Missouri," Talia answered. "St. Joseph, Michigan. I've lived in Michigan since I left the west coast."

"Are you retired?" Maggie pressed her.

"I am," Talia said. She seemed to relax a bit. "I retired from my last teaching post about five years ago."

"How long did you teach?" Maggie asked.

"Just over twenty-five years, long enough to set up my retirement," Talia said. Maggie tried to calculate how old she was and what she might have done with the rest of her time. "I was a bit of an activist before that."

"An activist for animal rights?" Maggie asked.

Talia nodded. "We traveled all over the world at one point," she said with a wistful smile. "We were in London one week and Paris for fashion week the next."

"Protesting the fashion industry?" Maggie asked her as she looked around the room.

"What do you need?" Talia asked her.

"Ricotta cheese, from the fridge," Maggie said. She was shocked when the woman stood up from her seat and retrieved the tub of ricotta from the fridge for her without a comment about where it came from. "Thank you."

"You're welcome," Talia said. "And yes, we protested the fashion industry. Believe it or not, I used to more than just harass old men about their recreational habits."

"Is that why you're here on this trip?" Maggie asked her casually. "Because you knew the men would be here on a fishing trip?"

"I'm here to enjoy a bird watching excursion," Talia said. "But the fact that the anglers were staying here might have influenced my decision to come."

Maggie wiped her hands off on a towel and turned around to face the older woman. "Do you really change hearts and minds by showing up and harassing people, as you put it? There just has to be a better way to share your message," she said.

"Are you some sort of animal rights convert all of a sudden?" Talia snapped.

Maggie shook her head. "Just a curious bystander, I suppose," she said lightly. "What did you do in London and in Paris?"

A slow smile crept across Talia's face. "We would find out where the fashion icons were dining," she said. "And we would wait for a cue from someone inside, usually a server or another diner who had gone there to keep an eye on them. And when they would get ready to leave after their hundred dollar dinner plates were cleared, we would stand just outside of the exit waiting for them to appear wrapped up in their precious fur coats." She appeared almost gleeful in her description.

"And when they stepped outside?" Maggie asked. She knew the answer already but wanted to hear and see Talia's reminiscing.

"We had buckets of red paint ready and when we were within range, we covered them from head to toe," she said. "The press was always there and always quick to snap a shot of some celebrity or another covered in red paint. Then one of us would give a quick statement while we were being hand-cuffed about how the rest of the world could now see that they had blood on their hands for wearing mink or whatever poor animal's fur."

"Why did you stop?" Maggie asked her. She opened the tub of ricotta cheese and spooned it into the pancake batter.

Talia shrugged her shoulders. "I got older, I guess. And I got tired of spending nights in jail and using what little money I might have had to bail myself out again," she said. "I decided that I could make more of a difference teaching the next generation about the evils of consumption and animal abuse."

"And now?"

"And now I am in search of any difference I can make at this point in my life, but it is hard when you get old, you know? Nobody takes you seriously," Talia said.

"It's almost like you have to do something big and brazen to be taken seriously, isn't it?" Maggie asked her.

Talia smirked and turned her full attention to her. Maggie expected a scathing insult about trying to trip her up and get her to confess to murder. She was surprised when Talia simply shrugged again and smiled.

"Something like that," she said and stood up and walked out of the kitchen.

"That was quite interesting," Ruby whispered when the woman had gone.

"It does shed a little bit of light on her character, doesn't it," Maggie said. She added lemon juice to the batter, and then carefully stirred in the lemon zest.

"If your blueberries have cooked down sufficiently, you need to let them cool before we serve them with the pancakes," Ruby instructed her.

Maggie was grateful for the distraction. Her attention had been so rapt on Talia's tales of her past life that she needed time to process the information. Without a doubt, the woman was at her very core, a passionate animal rights advocate. But she was also brash and annoying. She had no idea what might be going through the minds of the police chief and the county sheriff, but she was starting to wonder if the woman could have somehow been involved in the murder of Bob Jensen, even though she had been standing in front of her the whole time the unfortunate man died.

Maggie spooned the blueberry compote into six separate serving dishes. The multiple dishes would allow smaller amounts to cool down quickly, Ruby had told her. She set the large pan in the dishwasher and returned to the griddle on the stove. The pancakes added up quickly. Before long, she had filled three large platters with them. She moved the platters to the serving area next to the blueberries.

"There are a few bottles of maple syrup in the fridge," Ruby whispered to her. Maggie left to retrieve the syrup. Officer Kacy Hastings burst through the kitchen door from the outside as she passed by.

"Whoa, Officer Hastings," Maggie blurted. "Is everything okay?"

"No, it isn't," the officer said and rushed into the next room. She stopped and bent over a seated Gretchen as she passed her and whispered something in her ear. Maggie watched as Gretchen clutched her chest and nodded. Maggie waited until the officer had left the kitchen again and rushed to Gretchen's side.

"Are you alright, Gretchen?" she asked.

The older woman turned her body around in her chair and faced Maggie. "I don't know what's going on around here," she whispered. "That police officer just informed me that two of my guests have disappeared."

CHAPTER EIGHT

Maggie left Ruby in the kitchen at Gretchen's request and followed Officer Hastings to the formal living room in the front of the house.

"Miss Sharpe," the officer said when she saw her. "I am conducting official police business here. In fact, I was just on the phone with the police chief. I would rather you stay in the kitchen with your business partner."

"Gretchen asked for me to come and assist you," Maggie said.

"Why would she do that?"

"Because she said that you are searching for two house guests that have disappeared," Maggie said. "And because I grew up roaming around this house. I know exactly where all of the best hiding spots are."

"How is that supposed to help me?" Kacy asked, seemingly unsure of what was going on.

"If someone is trying to hide out somewhere in this house, I can help you find them," Maggie said. "If you start by telling me who it is we're looking for I might be able to help."

"Right now, Jack Wesley and Joe Lowman are missing," Kacy told her. "I have no idea how long they have been gone."

"What are their companions saying?"

"Nothing." The officer shook her head in obvious frustration. "I can't get some of them to even speak with me."

"Do you think they went somewhere together? As far as I understood it, Jack and Joe were not acquainted with each other outside of being here at the same time," Maggie said.

"That's the way we understood it, too," Kacy told her. "As far as we knew, they met the day before yesterday. The only thing they have in common is a mutual interest in trout fishing."

"And this excursion to the Ozarks for that purpose," Maggie said.

"Exactly. And Joe was Bob Jensen's best friend," Kacy said. She sighed and gazed up at the first set of stairs. "Why don't you show me where I should look first?"

Maggie smiled and led her up the steps to the second floor and then to the third. She ushered her through the narrow back hall and up another small flight to the attic. "I read stories about English children when I was a girl," she explained as they climbed. "I always called this part of the house 'the garret' because of that."

They walked across the creaky wooden floor and checked the nooks and crannies Maggie had used as hiding places when she was a child.

"Do you really expect we will find them up here?" Kacy asked her when they reached the middle of the large space.

Maggie shook her head. "That's the main reason I thought I might be useful to you," she said. "I doubt they are somewhere around here hiding, but you have to eliminate that possibility first. So, I thought I would take you around to absolutely any place I could think of in order to remove all doubt."

"I do appreciate it," Kacy said. "I don't always show my appreciation, but I mean it. I'm worried that I am going to screw this up. This is my first murder investigation."

"Just do what you know is right and you will be

fine," Maggie reassured her. "Now let's check out the back part of the attic so we can move down to the next floor and work our way down."

Maggie led her through the attic and pointed out spaces below windows and behind beams. They searched and found nothing in the garret.

"There are a couple of rooms Gretchen has turned into guest rooms on this level with a shared bathroom between them," Maggie explained. "But there is also a little known space behind the stairs that leads into a larger room where you can hide out of sight for a while." She led her down the hall and behind the steps. She opened a door to a smaller space that first appeared to be a closet, but the room opened up into an expansive space large enough for two more smaller bedrooms.

"This place is huge," Kacy said.

Maggie nodded. She pulled the string on an overhead light. "These new LED lights really illuminate things in here," she said. "When I was a girl this is where my uncle kept all of his dusty old books. It is one of my favorite rooms."

"Seems like it is more or less a storage room now," Kacy said. She shone the beam of her flashlight around in the corners.

"Wait," Maggie said. She reached for the officer's

arm and directed her back to the area behind an old table. "Look over there."

"What do you think you saw?" Kacy asked her. Her free hand hovered over her gun holster.

"Not a person, but something that seems out of place," Maggie said. "There!" She moved in front of the officer toward a large leather satchel shoved under a low coffee table.

"Why would you think that's important?"

"It looks like it was recently placed up here," Maggie said. "Look at how clean it is compared to everything else up here."

"You're pretty good at this, maybe even better than me." Kacy frowned. "This furniture could use a good dusting, but that bag is clean as a whistle."

"I wonder what it's doing there," Maggie said. She jumped when her phone chimed. She pulled it out and looked at the screen. "Sheriff Mission is downstairs."

"Does he know where this room is?" Kacy asked.

"He will when I tell him where to come," Maggie said. She typed the message into her phone quickly.

"I wonder what's holding up the chief?" Kacy asked.

Seconds later, Brett's heavy footsteps filled the

empty space. "All the way back here," Maggie said when she heard the door open.

"What's going on, honey?" he asked her, and then cleared his throat when he spotted the young police officer. "Officer Hastings, I didn't see you at first."

"Clearly," Maggie teased. She brushed his hand with her own when he passed her. "Over there, in the corner."

"The bag was recently placed there," Kacy said, sounding very official. "I was about to check it out for evidence."

"Shine your flashlight a little closer, Officer Hastings," Brett directed. He pushed the coffee table out of the way and knelt down on one knee. He pulled an ink pen from his shirt pocket and hooked it under the leather handles. When the bag was closer to him, he used the pen to push the top flap over and began to poke around inside. "Can you shine that light right inside there for me?"

"Let me get closer to you," Kacy said. She moved around the furniture and stood behind the satchel and pointed the flashlight directly inside. "What do you see?"

Brett didn't answer right away. He removed the cap of the pen and used the tip to extract something from inside the satchel.

NONE THE RISER   77

"What is it?" Maggie asked.

Brett sighed and held the object up into the beam of the flashlight. "It's a fishing lure," he said. "And if I am not mistaken, this one looks identical to the one someone plunged into Bob Jensen's jugular vein."

Kacy Hastings inhaled sharply. She opened her mouth to speak but was unable to get a single syllable out before the sound of a shrill scream from the floor below stopped her in her tracks.

"What was that?" Maggie gasped.

"I don't know, but we better get down there and find out," Brett said. He dropped the lure back in the satchel. "Officer Hastings, I want you to take out your cell phone and thoroughly photograph this area. Leave the satchel here for now and I'll come back for it once I figure out what's going on down there." He headed straight out of the room and down the stairs. Maggie followed quickly behind him.

CHAPTER NINE

Brett raced down the steps and Maggie followed behind him. Somewhere on her way down, she had made up her mind that Talia was the killer. She just needed the evidence to prove it.

But when they reached the living room and looked out the window, they found Chief Brooks Macklin standing over the animal rights activist. Maggie turned quickly away from the scene. It was clear that she had run into something sharp, forehead first. Maggie wandered around the house until she wound up in the kitchen, seated at a table across from Ruby who was actively comforting the homeowner.

"I know it's a lot for you to take, Gretchen," Ruby said to her. She held the woman's hand on her own. Her eyes locked with Maggie's.

Gretchen wasn't the only person in need of reassurance. "As soon as the sheriff gives the okay, why don't you have Albert drive you to the hotel in Hunter Springs?" Maggie suggested.

"That might not be a bad idea," Ruby agreed. She rose from the table and disappeared from the room.

"She'll be back," Maggie promised her.

"You girls have been through a lot yourselves lately," Gretchen told her. Maggie patted her hand and smiled. Despite the things happening around her, the fact that Gretchen referred to them as "girls" was not lost on her.

"We all have," Maggie said. She was surprised when Ruby returned followed by the groundskeeper and Brooks.

"I think we can all agree that the pair of you are not suspects in Ms. Henderson's death, or Bob Jensen's either, for that matter," Brooks said. "I have spoken with the sheriff, Gretchen. He suggested for you to allow Albert to take you to a hotel."

"But what about the Dogwood House? I have a house full of guests!"

"Yes, you do, and all of those guests are suspects in one way or the other," Brooks continued. "Neither Sheriff Mission nor I want to haul every one of them off to the county jail tonight. His solution is to spend the night here to keep an eye on everything," Brooks continued. "I will have one of my own officers posted here all night as well as the sheriff."

"What about the guests, though?" Gretchen asked again.

"I can stay," Maggie said before she could think better of it. "If the sheriff okays it. I can help make sure everyone has what they need."

Brooks nodded his head. "That was actually a thought the sheriff had as well," he said. "He will personally ensure Maggie's safety and distance from the crime scene, and my officers will help him keep an eye on your guests. We can figure something else out tomorrow."

"But it is still early in the day," Gretchen continued to protest.

"Yes, it is, ma'am," Albert said to her. "My suggestion is that we get our bags packed and get out of here so these good people can resume their interrogations. That way the right person gets put behind bars, and we get our lives back."

Gretchen nodded in agreement and stood up. She hesitated before she left the kitchen and headed to her bedroom. "Are you sure that you don't mind staying here, Maggie?"

"Of course not," she said with a reassuring smile.

In reality, she had considered staying overnight in Hunter Springs at Bradley's house. "I know my way around this place about as well as I do my own house." She turned to Brooks. "Is it alright if I go home for an overnight bag?"

"Of course," he said. "Just let Brett know what's going on."

Albert ushered Gretchen out of the kitchen toward her bedroom to pack. Maggie approached Ruby and was about to speak but stopped when she spotted two familiar figures through the kitchen window. "Joe! Jack!" She pointed at the window and turned to make sure Brooks saw the pair for himself.

Before she could say another word, the police chief was out the door with his service weapon trained on the pair. "Hands up," he commanded. Brett appeared in the kitchen a second later and joined him outside.

A few minutes later, the two men were seated on the porch in handcuffs.

"We haven't even been here," Jack cried out. "We were out early this morning fishing in Crawdad Creek!"

"He's telling you the truth," Joe called out next. "In fact, this was all my idea. I was planning on going myself this morning when Jack offered to accompany me."

"You both were told not to leave the bed and breakfast," Brett reminded them.

"We wouldn't have," Joe said. "But today was a special day. I have not missed a fishing trip on this date in over twenty years. My best friend Bob was usually with me. I went out for myself and for him, for old time's sake."

"You still left after you were told not to go anywhere," Brooks said.

"You can't order us to stay put," Jack argued. "Not unless we're under arrest."

"We can," Brett pointed out. "And we did."

"Man, listen to me," Joe was speaking again. "I just lost my best friend. Sue me if I want one more sunrise this year on a river bank fly fishing in his honor."

Maggie saw the too familiar white van arrive in the driveway on the far side of the property. She waited while the county medical coroner and his staff exited the van with their equipment and headed for the front of the large house.

"Why don't we gather the rest of breakfast and load everything into the dishwasher while they are busy outside?" Ruby suggested. "We should be finished in less than twenty minutes, and then you can run home after your things."

"And you can get home," Maggie whispered.

"Exactly," Ruby replied. She grabbed the tray closest to her and quickly began gathering the dishes. Maggie headed to the other side of the room and followed suit. Albert appeared as they loaded the dishwasher, carrying Gretchen's luggage. She had changed her clothes and hardened her face. She looked every bit the elderly passenger ready to board the Queen Mary II for a voyage to Europe.

Ruby packed up her dishes and the syrups and creamers and headed home, by way of the donut shop. Maggie pulled her phone out of her pocket and shot a text off to Brett that she was okay with staying the night at the bed and breakfast, and she was headed to her house to gather her things.

She made it to her car and out of the parking lot before the coroner's office was finished.

Maggie wondered if she had time to look Talia up when she got home. She was curious if there was more to the woman's activist past than she had alluded to.

CHAPTER TEN

Maggie drove her car back home. She called her son and told him what she was up to while she moved around her bathroom and gathered a few things for her overnight bag. Bradley aired his reservations about her plan to stay at the bed and breakfast but seemed satisfied when she informed him that Brett would be there along with officers from the Dogwood Mountain Police Department.

She filled up her overnight bag and double checked that her doors were locked before she headed to her car. She opened the door to set the bag on the back seat and gazed up at the sun shining high overhead.

"It must have been a nice morning for fishing," she said. She shut the door and got in behind the wheel, pausing before she headed back to the Dogwood House. She thought about the guests and about how the fishermen organized their trout fishing trip. She had even looked at the website where the men met and organized their excursions, although a membership was required to view the posts on the site's message board, which was where she understood such get togethers were often planned.

The men were not all friends in their real lives, that much she understood. Aside from Joe and Bob Jensen, most of the men only knew each other through the fishing website. There was no clear explanation why any one of them would want to kill Bob. She was at a complete loss for a reason, and she suspected that the police chief and sheriff were in the same boat.

But what she did not understand was the relationships among the members of the birdwatching expedition. The five women, actually four after the death of Talia, did not seem especially close. Maggie wondered if their get together was a similar circumstance, a group of individuals who had met and organized in an online space for people with similar interests.

The internet was truly a gift, she thought. Most of the people in either group had a few years on her, at least. Some were old enough to be her parents. It was both a blessing and a curse that they could connect online and then in person.

She backed out of her driveway after several moments of sitting still and musing on the events of the past few days. Getting back to the bed and breakfast was the next thing she needed to do. She was glad that Gretchen had enough faith in her to leave her home and business in her care.

She was also glad that the older woman had decided to heed the advice of others and leave while the murder scene could be processed and the people under her roof could be questioned and if necessary, dealt with accordingly.

When she arrived back at the large house, the white van from the medical examiner's office was gone. Maggie exhaled in relief. The last thing she wanted to see was another body of a person she had just seen and talked to getting pushed out under a white sheet.

Maggie parked her car on the far side of the first driveway, well out of the way of the other vehicles that filled the area, including the sheriff's car and two squad cars from the police department. She texted Brett that she had returned and planned to enter the house through the back kitchen door once again.

When she walked inside, she found the women from the birdwatching group. The four remaining women had pulled two bistro tables together in the middle of the room and surrounded it with their chairs. Without a word to them, Maggie set her bag down near the chairs against the far wall and returned to the main part of the kitchen. She washed her hands quickly in the sink and set the tea kettle on the stove and turned the fire on below it.

She located the tea mugs and a large tin filled with various tea bags from around the world. She suddenly found herself missing the kitchen of her donut shop, a place she knew like the back of her hand. The one thing she knew she could do was to keep the women well supplied with tea and coffee, but beyond that, she was unsure.

"Here we go, ladies," she said when the tea kettle sang after several minutes. Surprisingly, the group of four silently opened up and welcomed her within their ranks. Hannah reached behind her and pulled a fifth chair up for Maggie. "Oh, I don't want to disturb the rest of you."

"Nonsense," Hannah said. "I think we could all use another voice among us."

Maggie set the tea tin in the middle of the first table and left only long enough to retrieve a tea cup for herself. "When I was a little girl, there was a long table in this same space that was big enough to fit a family of twelve," she offered. "I thought that my aunt must entertain royalty when I was away."

A ripple of laughter filled the room. "What happened to your aunt?" Cissy asked.

"She passed away," Maggie said. "Aunt Marjorie was my great-aunt. She left me the donut shop and the small cottage I live in."

"Sounds like the two of you were close," Hannah said.

"We were very close," Maggie said. She gazed around the table. "Were any of you close to Talia?"

A couple of the women shifted uncomfortably in her seat.

"We didn't know her outside of our birdwatching group," Hannah said.

"Do you know each other?" Maggie asked, referring to Hannah and Cissy.

Cissy leaned forward and patted Hannah on the hand. "This dear lady helped me care for my older sister before she passed away," she said. "And her husband has been wonderful helping me care for things at my home."

Hannah smiled at Cissy and nodded. "I met Cissy while I was still working as a nurse," she said. "After

I retired, my husband and I just checked in on her once in a while."

"And the rest of you? Did you meet through the online group?"

"Yes, and that's how we all met Talia," Hannah said.

"Had any of you ever met Talia in person before?" Maggie asked.

"I met her once at a birdwatching conference," Hannah said. "But it was mainly online that we knew of her."

"And she was always such a character online," Cissy said, shaking her head. "I was a little hesitant to be around her in person."

"Why is that?" Maggie asked.

"Well, you saw the way she was at the donut shop," Hannah said. "That was her behavior online as well."

"She was not a very easy person to be around, in person or online, then," Maggie said.

"No, she was not," Cissy said. "But I can't understand why anyone would want to cause her any harm."

Hannah nodded. "I think she was a lonely woman," she said. "And she did know a lot about nature."

"Did you all arrive here before the men in the fishing group?"

"Only an hour or so," Hannah said. "We found out they were staying here right after we arrived."

"When did the tensions between the men and Talia start?" Maggie asked. She felt like she was getting nowhere with her questions.

"Almost right away," Cissy said. "The second she saw their fishing tackle."

"She was passionate and not very tactful or nice," Hannah said. "But Cissy is right. She did not deserve to be killed."

CHAPTER ELEVEN

Maggie set the tea mugs in the sink and threw the used bags in the trash. She replaced the tea tin on the shelf and washed the counter. The women remained seated at the table. They appeared content to sit and reminisce. However, Maggie was growing impatient and restless. She decided to step out on the porch and have a seat in one of the wooden chairs. Two sheriff deputies were milling around outside when she took her seat. It was just after lunch and she had no idea who had eaten and who had not, or who might expect a meal from the kitchen.

After just a few minutes, she decided to get up and head back inside. If nothing else, she could set out snacks on trays so the guests and the members of law enforcement could eat as they came and went through the kitchen.

Back inside the large kitchen, she removed the trays from the dishwasher and dried them off with a clean dish towel. She removed several blocks of cheese from the bottom of the large refrigerator. She sliced up the cheese and added sliced apples, ham, and salami. Gretchen had directed her to use whatever food she could find in the kitchen. Maggie searched the pantry for boxes of crackers to add to the trays. She set the food up on the serving counter and reloaded the dishwasher with the dirty dishes.

Once more, she found herself missing the donut shop kitchen and her routine.

Maggie stayed close to the kitchen as the afternoon wore on. The deputies she had seen outside left around four. Brett joined her in the kitchen and informed her that he was going home for a quick shower and a change of clothes. Brooks and Officer Hastings would remain behind for the time being.

While they were gone, Maggie decided to take her overnight bag to the small room on the third floor that she planned to sleep in. Brett planned to sleep downstairs where he could be close to the front door in case anyone else decided to leave. A police officer would remain on duty in the kitchen throughout the night.

Maggie ascended the stairs, passing the occupied rooms as she went along. When she reached the third floor, she selected the room closest to the stairs. She would have the bathroom to herself. Before she left the bedroom, her curiosity led her to the large, dimly lit room on the backside of the floor. She turned the flashlight on her phone and entered the long doorway, and then found her way to the light pull in the center of the room.

As soon as the overhead light switched on, she noticed the absence of the brown leather satchel behind the furniture against the far wall. Quickly she looked around the room for the bag. Careful not to touch anything, she searched every possible area she could for the satchel.

The bag was missing. Maggie pulled out her phone and immediately called Brett.

"Are you okay?" he asked as soon as he answered the call.

"I am, but I came up to the third floor to pick a room for the night," she said. "Brett, I decided to look in the back room again, just out of curiosity. And the satchel is missing."

"Are you sure?" he asked. She heard a car door slam and his car engine rev to life in the background.

"I looked all over the room," she said. "I don't see it anywhere."

"Stay there," he said. "I'll be back in five minutes."

Maggie hung up her phone and waited. She paced around the center of the room and waited for his return. She wanted to race downstairs and head out to her car and drive home. Her heart raced in her chest.

Someone had removed the satchel. She wondered if that same someone knew about the discovery of it by herself, Brett, and Officer Hastings.

She also wondered if that person might be aware of her whereabouts just then. She stopped walking. In her memory, she could hear her uncle's heavy footsteps on the upper floors of the house while she was downstairs with her aunt. If anyone had been listening, they would know that she was upstairs.

Her back was close to the doorway. The light from the single bulb did not illuminate the far corners of the room. Just outside the door she heard the floor creak. Maggie turned quickly around as soon as the door opened. She held her breath until Brett appeared directly in front of her.

"Oh, my gosh," she exclaimed and threw her arms around his neck. "I was just standing here wondering if the person who removed the satchel might be aware of the fact that I am up here."

"It's just me," Brett said. He pulled her fully into his arms and held her against his chest for a long moment. "I think we are going to need to conduct a room by room search for the bag. When that happens, you may need to just go home."

"But what about staying overnight?" she asked. She pushed herself back a bit, but his arms remained around her.

"I'm starting to think that we're going to need to move a couple of people to the county jail for their overnight accommodations," he said. "I need to speak with Brooks. What were you planning to do for dinner?"

"I had already figured that I would just order several entrees from Curley's and let them serve themselves," she said. "Do you want lasagna?"

"I'm in more of a pizza and salad sort of mood myself. Do you want to share one with me? It's not a date, but it is the closest thing we're going to get tonight."

"Unless you decide to send me home," Maggie said.

"That part is going to depend on the amount of resistance I get from the guests when they catch wind of our search for the bag," he said. "Why don't you go ahead and order the food. It's getting late enough that folks are probably starting to get hungry for real food. We don't need anyone getting too upset."

"Alright," Maggie said. "Do you want our normal order?"

"Order extra breadsticks this time," Brett said. "Last time you ate more than your half."

She shoved his arm playfully and headed for the door. She was silently grateful for his teasing. It helped her cope with the tension.

Maggie passed by her room for the night once more and headed for the second floor. She paused on the landing and gazed down the hallways before she ran all the way down to the bottom floor. As far as she could tell, no one was on the floor with her. She headed straight for the kitchen to place the order for the food but found herself alone when she entered. She called the Italian restaurant and turned her attention to the dishwasher once more.

It was close to seven when the delivery driver knocked on the back door. Maggie opened the door for her and waited while she made the trips to and from her vehicle with all of the food. She tipped the driver and set about putting the food and the disposable utensils out on the serving counter.

One by one the guests began to file into the kitchen, no doubt led by the aromas from the food. Maggie had set the pizza and salad aside she planned to share with Brett.

A single police officer accompanied the guests into the room. Maggie noted the absence of the police chief and the sheriff, but she made no comment about it. She could hear footsteps on the floor above her.

She was sure that Brett and Brooks were going through the guests' rooms in search of the leather satchel.

To her relief, no one else seemed aware of it. She wondered if that was the reason Brett had decided to let her stick around.

The women from the birdwatching group gathered on the right side of the kitchen. The fishermen settled into the other tables one by one. Joe stood close to the fridge with his plate in his hands and Jack sat alone. Unlike the women, the men appeared lost in their own thoughts.

Maggie noted the sound of someone on the stairs. She watched the group for signs that anyone else had noticed the noises from the other part of the house, but the group appeared to remain unaware of the activity above them.

She watched the clock while the guests finished

their meals. One by one the women rose and placed their plates in the large trash can. Hannah cast a weary smile in Maggie's direction. No doubt they wanted to leave the bed and breakfast and their spoiled vacation and head back to their own worlds. None of them complained, Maggie noticed. She was shocked by the women's resilience.

Most of the men remained mum as well, though she could feel the tension building among them. She wondered why the two men who had broken the rule and gone fishing earlier that morning were no longer sitting together.

Joe paced around near the appliances. He leaned against the cabinet and pushed his fork around in his food, took a bite, and then resumed his pattern of pacing. Maggie spotted the police officer watching him as he moved.

Above them, the movement had ceased. Inside the kitchen the guests were finishing their meals. Maggie wondered what would happen next. She wondered if she would wind up staying there overnight as planned, or if things were about to get out of hand.

She had to stay busy. The women had cared for their own trash, but the men had begun to shuffle around. Maggie moved from table to table and collected their used napkins and dinnerware. Some of the men returned to their tables after she cleared them off, while two others took to pacing in different parts of the kitchen.

Maggie wiped down the last table and headed back toward the sink. She stopped midway when she heard noise just outside of the back door. All at once, the door burst open. A large woman with striking red hair appeared in the doorway.

The police officer quickly crossed the room. He stood five feet from the woman. "Who are you and why are you here?" he demanded.

"I went to the front door and pounded on it, but no one would answer," the woman shouted. "Why are you all back here, anyway?"

"Who are you?" the officer asked her again.

The woman made a scene of setting her bags down on the floor and complaining about no one coming to the front door.

"I am not going to ask you again," the officer said sharply. "Who are you?"

The woman stopped fussing with her bags and looked up at the officer. Her eyes darted around the room. "My name is Lois Jensen," she said. "I'm Bob Jensen's wife."

Before another word was spoken, Brett and Brooks descended the stairs in a thunder of footsteps.

They appeared in the kitchen in a rush. Brett held the brown leather satchel in his hand.

Lois glanced around the room and gasped when she spotted Joe. "What on earth are you doing here?" she shouted.

"I'm on a fishing trip," Joe stammered.

Lois Jensen's head swiveled toward the sheriff and the police chief for the first time. "And why do you have my husband's bag? That is not supposed to leave his sight!"

As soon as Lois identified the bag, Joe dropped his spaghetti on the floor of the kitchen and rushed around the tables and down the hall toward the master bedroom suite. Brett shoved the bag into the arms of the waiting police officer and took off running after him. Brooks was a step behind him.

"Everyone, remain where you are," the police officer shouted. All movement in the kitchen stopped. Another officer appeared in the doorway. Maggie fought the temptation to run down the hallway after the men. Lois wavered slightly on her feet and Maggie glanced at the police officer and rushed to her side. She shoved an empty chair under her just as she fell back into it.

Seconds later, a series of shouts came from the side of the house. Both police officers placed their hands on their weapons and watched as Brooks appeared again leading a now handcuffed Joe with him. Brett followed them back into the kitchen.

"I don't understand what is going on," Lois said quietly. She sniffed loudly and began to softly cry. "Why is that man here?"

"He was on a trout fishing excursion like the rest of us," Jack said. "He said he was your husband's best friend."

Lois wiped her eyes and stood up. She pointed a shaking finger at the handcuffed man. "You are not my husband's friend! You are a liar and a cheat! You preyed on his good nature and took advantage of him, and I will not tolerate it!"

CHAPTER TWELVE

Maggie twisted the top of the overly stuffed trash bag and secured the twist tie around it. She walked through the kitchen door of the large house and crossed the porch to the trash bins outside, picked up the metal lid, and shoved the bag inside.

She glanced around the outside before heading back in the house. The driveway was empty except for a couple of vehicles. Once Joe Lowman had been hauled off to jail, the other guests had been given the go ahead to leave. Maggie was slightly shocked by their speed when they returned to their rooms to packs and their equally hasty exits.

But then, their getaway had been beyond ruined by two murders, unofficial house arrest, and the dramatic conclusion. By then, Joe was cooling his heels in the county jail. The bag of lures had been removed from the large house and placed into police custody for evidence. Lois Jensen had been removed by ambulance after she passed out in the middle of the kitchen floor.

"I wondered if you were still here," Ruby called to her from the yard.

"I didn't see you come up," Maggie said and smiled. She was glad to see a friendly face.

"I thought you could use a hand putting things back in order before Gretchen returns," Ruby said.

Maggie sighed and hung her head. "You know me too well."

Ruby followed her back inside the house. Maggie locked the door behind them. "It's starting to feel like a house of horrors around here," she said.

"It's almost dark outside," Ruby said. "Given what you have been through, I don't blame you for locking the door."

"I really don't have much more to do," Maggie said. "But I am so glad that you are here."

"When is Gretchen supposed to be back?"

"She isn't sure if she plans to be back tonight or if she will just wait until the morning," Maggie said. "Albert will be here tonight, though."

"Are you sure you don't want to spend the night?" Ruby teased.

Maggie shook her head. "You couldn't pay me to sleep here," she said.

"What happened, exactly?" Ruby asked. She took the new trash bag from Maggie and placed it in the trash can.

"Joe took off running and Brooks caught him first," Maggie said with a grin. "I am going to give Brett such a hard time about that, you know."

"I meant with the widow, Lois," Ruby said. "How did she end up in the hospital?"

"Joe confessed to both murders while he was being walked out of the kitchen," Maggie said. "It was the most dramatic thing I have ever seen. He admitted that he lied to Bob about some dispute they had years ago and had come on the trip with him. Apparently Bob kept the fact that Joe was coming on the trip from his wife."

"But why did she faint?"

"Because part of his confession revealed that the fishing lure he had used to kill Bob with was one of her father's antique lures," Maggie explained. "That was what the entire event was all about. Apparently Joe and Bob had been friends and fishing buddies twenty years ago."

"Until what happened?" Ruby asked.

"Until they got into a dispute about a fishing lure and who it belonged to," Maggie said. "Brett told me that the fight ended their relationship. Bob became a renowned collector in that time and Joe was jealous of the fact that he had been able to acquire so many pieces through the years. He admitted that he had made amends just to get him on the trip and get this special lure back from him. That's why he took the leather satchel out of Bob's room and hid it upstairs. He was trying to find the lure. And when he couldn't find it, he took the six-segmented lure Lois's father had given him and shoved it into his neck at the donut shop."

"What about the woman, the animal rights lady? Why kill her?" Ruby asked.

"I think that was a simple case of being in the wrong place at the wrong time," Maggie said. "When I went upstairs and checked out the spare room once again, I noticed that it had been removed. I let Brett know right away that the bag was missing. Someone had obviously removed it."

"I still don't understand," Ruby said.

"The bag was essential to the killer. In this case, it was Joe," Maggie said. "Talia happened to be outside when Joe was walking by with the bag. He killed her instantly so she couldn't identify him with the bag or ask any questions."

"What about the other guy, the one who sneaked out with him to go fishing this morning?" Ruby asked. "I thought he was his alibi."

"Turns out they weren't together the entire time," Maggie said. "But Jack was a little shy about bringing that up. I noticed how mum he became when they got back. I think he was beginning to suspect Joe, and he was afraid that he might wind up with a lure in his neck too."

Ruby settled into one of the chairs and shook her head. "Two deaths over a fishing lure. What a waste."

"I agree with you," Maggie said. "And all of these people are forever traumatized because of Joe's jealousy. That's why the wife passed out. She hadn't been informed how her husband had died."

"What a way to find out," Ruby said.

"No kidding," Maggie said. "I wonder if any of these people will ever enjoy their hobbies again."

"I'm never going fishing again," Ruby said. "After what we saw at work, I don't care to ever touch a fish hook another time in my life."

If you enjoyed None the Riser, check out the next book in the series, Starch Enemy, today!

AUTHOR'S NOTE

I'd love to hear your thoughts on my books, the storylines, and anything else that you'd like to comment on—reader feedback is very important to me. My contact information, along with some other helpful links, is listed on the next page. If you'd like to be on my list of "folks to contact" with updates, release and sales notifications, etc.… just shoot me an email and let me know. Thanks for reading!

Also…

… if you're looking for more great reads, Summer Prescott Books publishes several popular series by outstanding Cozy Mystery authors.

CONTACT SUMMER PRESCOTT BOOKS PUBLISHING

Blog and Book Catalog: http://summerprescottbooks.com

Email: summer.prescott.cozies@gmail.com

And...be sure to check out the Summer Prescott Cozy Mysteries fan page and Summer Prescott Books Publishing Page on Facebook – let's be friends!

To sign up for our fun and exciting newsletter, which will give you opportunities to win prizes and swag, enter contests, and be the first to know about New Releases, click here: http://summerprescottbooks.com

Made in United States
North Haven, CT
15 March 2023

34102874R00065